Dedicated to you. May your cuts always be cold.

Cold Cuts
Winter Horrors Book Two
Written By: B. Humphrey

Copyright © 2024 by B. Humphrey All rights reserved. No part of this book may be reproduced or transmitted in any form or by any means without the prior written permission of the author, except for the use of brief quotations in a book review.

All characters, movies, songs, and fictional scenarios belong to their original creators and trademark owners respectfully.

This is a work of fiction. Names, characters, places, and incidents are the product of the author's imagination or used fictitiously. Any resemblance to actual persons, living or dead, or actual events is purely coincidental.

Chapter One: The Lure of the Wilderness

The forest stretched out before them, a boundless expanse of white, silent and perfect. Snow blanketed the earth in a way that felt like a dream—a place that time and footsteps had left untouched. Every tree was coated in frost, branches bending beneath their icy load, and the air had a sharpness to it, a crispness that felt pure. This was what had drawn them here, the unspoiled beauty of nature in its rawest form, stripped bare by the cold.

Jake led the way, his boots crunching over the frozen ground as he turned back to the group with a grin. "Feels like we're stepping into another world, huh?"

Ben, his best friend, jogged up to his side, his breath visible in white puffs as he took in the scenery. "I feel like we should be filming a commercial or something," he joked. "You know, 'Live Life Untamed' or whatever."

Behind them, Sarah rolled her eyes, but a smile tugged at her lips. She was captivated by the view as much as anyone, and her fingers were already itching to pull out her sketchbook. She nudged her sister, Claire, who was silent as usual, her wide eyes darting from shadow to shadow between the trees.

The four of them were bundled against the cold, their scarves pulled up to their noses, hats tugged low, and still, the chill managed to slip through, biting at their skin like tiny needles.

But the cold was a part of it, Jake thought. It made the world feel clean, untouched by anything but snow and silence.

They wandered off the main trail, deeper into the woods where the snow was thicker, undisturbed by previous hikers. Each step felt like carving a path into a forgotten realm, one hidden from the rest of the world. For a while, they talked and laughed, the sounds bright and loud against the quiet.

Yet, as they moved deeper, even Ben started to grow quiet. The trees here were thicker, the shadows longer, and the silence somehow more profound. It was as if the forest had swallowed every sound, every breath, leaving only the muffled crunch of their footsteps.

"I've never been anywhere so...quiet," Sarah whispered, looking around. The silence seemed to press in on them, growing heavier with each step. "It's like the trees are listening."

Jake chuckled, though the sound was subdued. "Creeping yourself out already? We just got here."

"Maybe," Sarah said with a small laugh, but her eyes didn't leave the shadows.

Claire stayed close to her sister, her gloved hand wrapped around the strap of her backpack. She'd been quiet since they'd left the car, her gaze distant, thoughtful. Every so often, she'd stop, her head tilted as if she was listening to something the others couldn't hear.

They found a small clearing, a circle of untouched snow that seemed made for them. Jake dropped his backpack and looked around. "Perfect spot to set up camp, don't you think?"

The others agreed, and soon they were unpacking, pitching their tents in the heart of the clearing, laughing and shoving each other to stay warm. It felt like an adventure—cold, uncomfortable, but thrilling in a way they hadn't expected.

The forest around them seemed to hold its breath as night fell, the pale light fading, leaving only the faint glow of their flashlights. They huddled around a small fire, the flames casting long shadows that danced across the trees. Above them, the sky was clear, the stars sharp and bright, each one a pinprick in the deep, dark blue.

As they ate, their laughter grew quiet, and a strange hush settled over them. They sat in silence, listening to the crackle of the fire, the occasional creak of a tree bending under the weight of snow.

Ben broke the silence first, glancing around with a half-smile. "Does anyone else feel like we're being watched?"

Sarah shivered, pulling her blanket tighter around her shoulders. "It's the forest. Everything feels like it's watching."

"It's beautiful, though," Claire said softly, her gaze fixed on a spot just beyond the trees where the firelight couldn't reach. "But...different. Like it's waiting for something."

Jake reached over and ruffled her hat, smiling to break the tension. "I think it's just that we're not used to all this quiet. Back home, there's always noise, always something going on."

But even he couldn't shake the feeling that there was something else out there. The shadows felt too thick, the silence too deep. Every so often, he thought he saw movement at the edge of the firelight—a quick, darting shadow that disappeared the second he tried to focus on it.

The fire died down, and one by one, they crawled into their tents, leaving the clearing in darkness. Jake lay awake, listening to the others' slow, steady breathing. Outside, the forest was silent, so silent he could almost hear his own heartbeat.

Jake drifted in and out of sleep, haunted by strange, disjointed dreams. He saw the forest, stretching endlessly, the trees shifting and bending as if alive. The snow glittered under a strange, pale light, and in the distance, he heard a voice—soft, calling to him, but when he tried to move, he couldn't. His limbs were heavy, his body frozen in place as the voice grew closer, louder.

He woke with a start, his breath coming fast, his heart pounding. The tent was dark, and outside, the world was silent. But something was wrong—he could feel it, a prickling sensation at the back of his neck, a cold that seemed to seep into his bones.

And then he heard a faint, almost imperceptible whisper. It drifted through the trees, a sound that was barely there, a sound that shouldn't be there.

Jake lay still, straining to hear, his body tense. The whisper faded, replaced by the soft, almost rhythmic creaking of branches in the wind. He told himself it was nothing, just the sounds of the forest, but the feeling lingered, a weight pressing down on him.

When they woke, the clearing was blanketed in a fresh layer of snow, and their tracks from the day before had vanished, as though they'd never been there at all. They packed up in silence, each of them casting uneasy glances toward the trees.

As they started back toward the trail, Claire paused, looking back at the clearing, her face pale.

"What is it?" Sarah asked, noticing her sister's expression.

Claire shook her head, but her eyes were wide, her voice barely a whisper. "I...thought I saw someone standing there. Just for a second."

The others exchanged nervous glances, but no one spoke. They moved quickly, their steps faster than before, eager to put distance between themselves and the clearing.

Yet, as they walked, the feeling didn't leave them. The silence followed, pressing in close, and every so often, one of them would glance back, half-expecting to see a shadow slipping through the trees.

But the forest was empty. Silent. As if waiting for them to come back.

Chapter Two: Strange Signs

The sun was a dull, silver disc as it climbed the sky, casting a pale light over the snow-covered forest. Everything around them was coated in frost, each branch and leaf frozen in place, as though the world had been paused mid-breath. It was stunningly beautiful, but as they trudged deeper, something in that beauty began to feel wrong, like a mask covering something darker.

Jake led the way, his boots crunching over the snow, leaving deep, jagged prints behind him. Sarah followed, her eyes wide as she took in the landscape, her sketchbook clutched to her chest. She'd been quiet since they'd left the campsite, her face thoughtful, as if something about the forest bothered her but she couldn't quite put her finger on it.

"Anyone else getting the feeling we're the only people who've ever been here?" Ben asked, spinning in a slow circle, his scarf trailing behind him. He laughed, but it was a nervous sound, thin and fragile against the silence.

"Or the only ones dumb enough to come this far out in the cold," Sarah replied, a slight smile tugging at her lips. She looked over at her sister, who had been trailing behind, her gaze fixed on something just beyond the line of trees.

"What is it, Claire?" she asked, glancing back.

Claire frowned, tilting her head slightly, as if listening to something only she could hear. "I thought...I thought I saw something. Probably just my eyes playing tricks."

"Probably," Jake said, though he found himself glancing in the same direction, squinting into the shadows.

The snow here was deep and untouched, blanketing the forest floor in an unbroken expanse of white. Yet, as they moved forward, they began to notice things that didn't quite fit. A tree with strange markings carved into its bark, symbols that twisted and curled like vines. Another tree with its branches stripped bare, each limb stark and skeletal against the sky.

Sarah pulled out her sketchbook, tracing the symbols with her fingers before she started drawing. "Look at these...they almost look like words."

"Who'd bother to carve something all the way out here?" Ben asked, leaning in for a closer look. He ran a gloved finger over the marks, his brow furrowing.

"Maybe it's some kind of hiker's code?" Jake offered, though he didn't believe it. There was something about the marks that felt old, as if they'd been there long before anyone could remember.

They continued on, the silence pressing down around them, until they reached a small clearing where the snow had melted away, leaving the ground bare and dark. Jake stopped, staring at the strange circle of earth that seemed untouched by the cold.

"What...is this?" he murmured, feeling a shiver that had nothing to do with the temperature.

Sarah knelt down, her fingers grazing the bare ground. It was damp, warm even, as if some hidden heat was rising up from beneath. She looked up at Jake, her face pale. "It's like the snow can't touch it."

Ben laughed, a hollow sound that felt out of place. "What, you think the ground's haunted?"

"No," Sarah replied, though her voice was uncertain. "It's just...strange."

They moved on, leaving the circle behind, but the unease lingered, settling in their stomachs like stones. The forest felt different now, its beauty tinged with something darker. Every tree seemed to lean toward them.

As the sun began to dip behind the trees, casting long, skeletal shadows across the snow, they came across something even stranger. Animal bones, scattered in a rough circle on the ground, their pale surfaces gleaming against the dark earth.

Claire stopped dead, her face going pale. "Is that...?"

"Bones," Jake said, his voice barely a whisper. He knelt down, examining the circle. The bones were small, likely from a rabbit or a fox, but the way they were arranged felt deliberate, as if someone had placed them there with a purpose.

"What kind of animal does that?" Ben asked, his voice shaky.

"An animal didn't do this," Sarah said, her eyes wide. She looked around, as if expecting something to jump out at them from the shadows. "This was...someone else."

Jake felt a chill creep down his spine, but he forced a laugh, trying to break the tension. "Probably some hiker messing around, trying to freak people out."

Ben chuckled, though his laugh was thin and unsteady. "Well, it's working."

They left the bones behind, but every so often, one of them would glance back, half-expecting to see someone following them, a shadow slipping through the trees.

As they made their way back to camp, the silence seemed to grow heavier, pressing down around them until every sound felt muffled, swallowed by the snow. By the time they reached the clearing, night had fallen, and the world was bathed in a deep, eerie blue. The trees loomed above them like dark giants, their branches arching overhead like the fingers of a hand reaching out to snatch them up.

The fire crackled in the center of the camp, casting long shadows that danced over the snow. They huddled around it, silent, each of them lost in their own thoughts. The warmth of the flames was comforting, but it didn't reach far, leaving the edges of the clearing cloaked in darkness.

As they ate, Jake found himself glancing over his shoulder, his eyes scanning the shadows. He couldn't shake the feeling that they weren't alone, that something was watching them from the trees. Every so often, he thought he saw movement—a flicker of shadow, a quick flash of something pale.

"You okay, Jake?" Sarah asked, her voice soft.

He forced a smile, nodding. "Yeah. Just...tired, I guess."

But even as he said it, he couldn't shake the feeling of being watched. It was an oppressive, almost physical sensation, like a weight pressing down on his shoulders, urging him to run, to get out while he still could.

Ben tried to lighten the mood, telling a story about a haunted cabin he'd heard about in town, but his voice was thin, lacking its usual bravado. The others laughed, but the sound was hollow, echoing into the silence before fading away.

In the dead of night, as they lay in their tents, the sound began—a faint, rhythmic scratching, like claws against bark. Jake lay still, his eyes wide, his breath coming in short, sharp bursts. The sound was coming from outside, moving around the edge of the clearing, circling them like a predator stalking its prey.

Sarah shifted beside him, her hand reaching for his. "Do you hear that?" she whispered.

He nodded, his grip tightening around her fingers. "Yeah."

The scratching grew louder, closer, moving in irregular patterns that seemed to come from all directions. It was as if something was pacing around them, studying them, deciding when to strike.

The sound stopped suddenly, leaving the clearing in silence. They lay there, holding their breath, waiting, but nothing happened. After a long, tense moment, they finally allowed themselves to relax, letting out shaky breaths.

But as they drifted back to sleep, a new sound filled the air—a faint whisper, soft and eerie, drifting through the trees like the last remnants of a dying wind. It was a sound that didn't belong, a sound that seemed to come from deep within the forest, carrying with it a sense of ancient, unknowable dread.

Jake lay awake, listening to the whisper, his heart pounding. He couldn't understand the words, but he knew, somehow, that it was a warning.

And in that moment, he realized the forest was more than just trees and snow. It was something alive, something watching, something waiting.

Chapter Three: The Spore's Hold

The forest greeted them with an almost unnatural stillness the next morning, as if the snow-covered world around them were holding its breath. The sky was a pale gray, the light diffused and dull, casting everything in a ghostly hue. Each tree was frosted white, reaching upward in jagged formations, their branches like thin arms grasping at the sky.

Jake rubbed his hands together, blowing into them to chase away the chill that seemed to have settled into his bones. It wasn't just the cold; it was something deeper, a feeling that had crept into him during the night. He'd barely slept, haunted by strange dreams that lingered on the edge of his mind, fading in and out like the echo of a forgotten melody.

The others weren't much better off. Sarah's eyes were red-rimmed, her face pale, and Claire stood silently, her gaze distant, as though she were looking past the trees to something only she could see. Ben tried to joke, but his laughter was hollow, lacking its usual bravado.

They packed up in silence, the chill settling between them like an unspoken presence. As they walked, Jake felt a strange sensation—a tightness in his limbs, as if his muscles were stiffening. He shook it off, blaming the cold, but as they moved deeper into the forest, the feeling grew worse. His arms felt heavy, his steps sluggish.

"Anyone else feel...weird?" he asked, forcing a laugh. But his voice sounded thin, strained.

Sarah gave him a sidelong glance, her brow furrowed. "Yeah. I thought it was just the cold, but..." She trailed off, rubbing her arms. "It's like everything's heavier."

Ben shrugged, trying to play it off, but even he couldn't hide the discomfort in his eyes. "Maybe we're just out of shape," he said, but there was a flicker of fear in his voice.

Claire stayed silent, her gaze fixed on the ground as they walked. She looked pale, her breaths coming in shallow gasps. Her movements were slow, as if she were walking through water.

The forest felt denser here, the trees packed close together, their branches interwoven like the bars of a cage. Snow clung to every surface, muffling their footsteps, and the only sounds were their ragged breaths and the occasional creak of a branch under the weight of ice.

As they continued, the tightness in Jake's limbs grew worse, spreading through his body like a slow, creeping sickness. His legs felt like lead, his arms heavy and unresponsive. Every step was a struggle, a silent battle against the weight pressing down on him.

They paused to catch their breath, leaning against a cluster of trees, and Sarah sank down onto a fallen log, her face pale. "Something's...wrong," she whispered, glancing around. "This isn't normal."

"Maybe we should turn back," Jake said, though the words felt like a betrayal. He didn't want to admit the fear gnawing at him, didn't want to acknowledge the growing certainty that something terrible was lurking just beyond their sight.

Ben shook his head, his face set in a determined scowl. "We've come this far. I say we keep going."

Claire looked up, her eyes wide and frightened. "What if we can't get out?"

The question hung in the air, a silent acknowledgment of the dread that had settled over them. They all felt it—the sense of being trapped, of something waiting for them in the shadows.

Jake forced a smile, trying to shake off the fear. "We're just tired. Once we get moving, we'll feel better."

But as they pushed forward, the feeling only grew worse. The forest seemed to close in around them, the trees pressing closer, their branches arching overhead like a twisted canopy. Shadows shifted in the corners of their vision, and every so often, Jake thought he saw movement—a flicker of something pale and thin slipping between the trees.

Hours passed in silence, the weight in their limbs growing heavier, their breaths coming in shallow gasps. The trail they'd followed had long since vanished, swallowed by the snow, leaving them in a landscape that felt strange and alien, as if the forest itself had changed around them.

Sarah stopped suddenly, her face pale. "We've...we've been here before."

Jake glanced around, his stomach twisting as he recognized the trees around them. They were in the same clearing they'd passed an hour ago, the same twisted branches looming above them like skeletal arms.

"How is that possible?" Ben asked, his voice thin and strained.

"We must have...we must have taken a wrong turn," Jake said, but the words sounded hollow, even to him. He could feel the fear settling in his chest, a cold, creeping dread that gnawed at the edges of his mind.

They tried again, turning in a new direction, but the forest seemed to shift around them, the trees rearranging themselves like pieces on a board. Every path they took led them back to the same spot, the same clearing with its twisted branches and deep shadows.

As the day wore on, the symptoms grew worse. Jake's arms felt numb, his legs heavy and unresponsive. Every step was a struggle, his muscles refusing to obey him. He could see the same exhaustion in the others—the same stiffness in their movements, the same pale, frightened expressions.

Claire stumbled, falling to her knees, and Sarah rushed to help her, her face etched with worry. "Claire, are you okay?" Claire looked up, her face pale and drawn. "I...I can't move my legs."

The words sent a chill through them, a silent confirmation of what they'd all been fearing. They were trapped, their bodies betraying them, held captive by a force they couldn't see or understand.

Jake knelt beside her, his hand on her shoulder. "It's okay, we'll get out of here. We just need to keep moving."

But even as he said it, he could feel the weight pressing down on him, the tightness in his muscles growing worse. His arms felt like lead, his legs unresponsive, as though some unseen force were binding him in place.

They tried to keep going, but their progress was slow, each step a battle against the weight that held them down. The forest loomed around them, silent and indifferent, its shadows deepening as the light began to fade.

As they stumbled forward, Jake saw something ahead—a figure standing in the shadows, its form pale and thin, almost skeletal. He froze, his heart pounding, as the figure stepped forward, its face hidden in shadow.

The others stopped, following his gaze, their faces pale with fear. The figure was watching them, its head tilted at an unnatural angle, its limbs long and twisted. It took a step forward, its movements slow and deliberate, and they could see its eyes—dark, sunken, and filled with a hunger that sent a shiver down their spines.

Jake tried to speak, but the words caught in his throat, his voice choked with terror. The figure took another step, its body swaying as it moved, and he felt the weight pressing down on him, holding him in place, refusing to let him run.

"Go...back..." the figure whispered, its voice barely more than a breath. The words sent a chill through him, a warning laced with something darker, something malevolent.

And then, just as suddenly as it had appeared, the figure melted back into the shadows, vanishing among the trees. The silence returned, pressing down on them, filling the clearing with an oppressive weight that made it hard to breathe.

They stood there, frozen, the fear settling over them like a blanket of snow. Each of them knew, in that moment, that they were trapped, held captive by the forest and the unseen force that lurked within it.

Chapter Four: The Family

Jake stirred, his senses coming back to him slowly, as if he were drifting up from a dark, endless sea. At first, he felt nothing. He was dimly aware of cold—a numbing chill that bit through his clothes and seemed to seep into his bones. When he finally opened his eyes, he found himself half-buried in snow, his body wedged in a deep drift, only his head and shoulders visible. Snow caked his hair, icy flecks settling on his lashes, and his face burned with a frozen ache.

He tried to move, but his limbs wouldn't obey him. Panic surged, his mind racing, but his body stayed stubbornly still, as if it were held by invisible chains. All around him, the forest loomed, silent and indifferent, the trees rising like dark pillars against the pale sky.

He wasn't alone.

Scattered around him were the others, half-submerged in the snow, their faces pale and wide-eyed with terror. They, too, were paralyzed, their eyes darting wildly, mouths slightly open as they struggled to speak, to scream, to do anything. But there was only silence, their breath forming small clouds that hung in the frigid air.

Then they saw them—the family.

They moved out of the trees in a slow, lumbering shuffle, their figures twisted and deformed, like something out of a nightmare. The father was massive, broad-shouldered and hunched, with one arm hanging at an odd angle and his face half-hidden by tufts of wiry hair that stuck out from beneath a battered fur hat. The mother, tall and gaunt, was a shadow beside him, her face gaunt and sallow, one eye staring blankly while the other drooped as if melted.

Three children trailed after them, each more horrifying than the last. The eldest, a teenage boy with a hunched back and a lopsided grin, dragged a length of rusted chain behind him, his eyes darting around with a hungry gleam. The middle child, a boy around ten, had a swollen face covered in scars, his nose little more than a flattened lump, his mouth twisted in a permanent sneer. And then there was the youngest—a little girl, no more than six, her face disturbingly doll-like, with wide, vacant eyes that held no hint of innocence.

Jake's mind screamed for him to move, to get up and run, but his body remained still, locked in place by the spore's hold.

The family advanced, stopping a few feet from the group. They studied their prey with interest, their heads tilting in slow, jerky movements. The father grunted, a low, guttural sound, and the mother responded with a shrill giggle that sent a shiver down Jake's spine.

Then, the little girl stepped forward, her tiny hands gripping something long and gleaming—a machete, its edge jagged and chipped. She approached Jake, her wide eyes fixed on him, a faint smile curving her lips. Her face was twisted, malformed, with one side slightly drooping, giving her an unsettling, lopsided look.

The world narrowed to her, to the sick anticipation in her gaze, the gleam of the blade in her small, steady hands.

Jake's mind screamed, his instincts flaring with a need to escape, to fight, but his body remained locked in place, his muscles as frozen as the snow around him. His breath came in short, shallow gasps, visible in faint clouds that drifted up and vanished in the cold air.

The little girl with the machete stepped forward, her eyes fixed on Jake with an eerie intensity. She tilted her head, her face a strange, unnatural mask of curiosity and cruelty. Her tiny hands gripped the hilt of the machete tightly, the blade catching the dim light as she raised it above her head.

Without a word, without a sound, she brought the machete down in a brutal arc, the jagged edge biting into Jake's arm with a sickening crunch. His flesh split, blood spurting into the snow, staining it a vivid red. The pain was immediate, sharp and blinding, but he was trapped, unable to scream, unable to move as she hacked at his arm again, the blade tearing through flesh and bone with each swing.

The others could only watch, their eyes wide with horror, their breaths coming in gasps as they witnessed the horror unfolding before them. Sarah's face was a mask of terror, her body rigid in the snow, her mind screaming with the helplessness of being unable to reach out, to stop what was happening.

The girl hacked again, her movements clumsy but determined, her little arms working with a terrifying eagerness as she severed Jake's arm. Finally, with a final, brutal swing, the arm came free, hanging loosely in her tiny hands, dripping blood onto the snow.

She looked at the severed limb, her expression one of fascination and glee. She lifted the arm, swinging it in the air, the blood splattering across Jake's face, painting the snow in a grim arc of red. Her vacant eyes sparkled with a twisted joy as she danced around him, waving the arm like a grisly trophy, her mouth curving into a mockery of a smile.

The father grunted in approval, his twisted grin stretching wider as he watched his youngest play with her prize. The mother let out a shrill giggle, her one good eye gleaming with a sick pride as she took in the terror on her victims' faces.

The other children began to move forward, their hands reaching for the paralyzed group, their faces alight with anticipation. They dragged the group members through the snow, spreading them out like trophies, each victim half-buried in the cold, watching in horror as the nightmare unfolded.

Jake's mind was a blur of pain and fear, his vision swimming as the little girl danced around him, his severed arm held high like a twisted prize. He could feel the weight of his own blood, warm and sticky, seeping into the snow, the cold biting at the raw, open wound.

One by one, the family gathered around, each of them inspecting the captured prey, their hands reaching out to touch, to prod, their twisted faces alight with cruel glee. The father leaned in close to Jake, his hot, rancid breath washing over him as he grunted, his eyes glinting with a sick satisfaction.

The mother whispered something to her children, her voice soft and low, and they moved forward, their hands eager, their faces contorted with excitement. They grabbed Jake and his friends, dragging them deeper into the forest, their bodies limp and heavy, leaving a trail of blood in the snow.

In the shadows, the family moved like animals, their twisted forms silhouetted against the pale sky, their voices low and guttural as they worked, each of them grinning, each of them reveling in the suffering they inflicted.

And as Jake's vision faded, he could see the little girl, still dancing, still waving his severed arm in the air, her laughter silent but chilling, her wide eyes empty and dark.

Chapter Five: The Ritual of Pain

The forest felt darker, denser, as the family dragged their captives through the snow, deeper into the twisted heart of the wilderness. The shadows cast by the trees stretched longer, clawing at the snow-covered ground, and the once serene, untouched beauty of the forest had turned malevolent, as if it, too, hungered for the terror and pain echoing between the trunks.

The father, a hulking figure with a twisted face and gnarled hands, led the way, his heavy boots crunching into the snow. The mother followed, her skeletal form swaying with a strange, jerky grace, her one good eye gleaming as she looked back at the helpless captives dragged through the snow.

Jake, Sarah, Ben, and Claire were pulled through the forest like sacks of meat, their bodies limp, leaving trails of blood and broken snow in their wake. Each of them struggled in their minds, their instincts screaming at them to move, to fight, but the spore held them fast, their muscles frozen, only their eyes darting frantically as they tried to take in their surroundings.

Eventually, they reached a clearing surrounded by trees, their twisted branches arching above in a tangled web. In the center, a makeshift fire pit crackled with flames, its embers casting an eerie glow over the family's gaunt, deformed faces. A few splintered logs were arranged around the fire, as though this place was a gathering spot, a place where the family came to "celebrate" their rituals.

The father grunted, his voice low and guttural, a signal to his children. They moved quickly, their twisted forms shifting in the firelight, their hands rough and strong as they dragged the captives to separate spots around the fire, binding each one tightly with rope. The bindings bit into their skin, the coarse material rough and cold, further immobilizing them even as their limbs remained lifeless.

The mother moved from one captive to the next, her bony fingers touching their faces, her touch like ice, slow and deliberate as if savoring each one. Her mouth twisted into a smile that was more a grimace, her eyes flaring with a mixture of hunger and delight.

When she reached Ben, she paused, her fingers tracing a line along his cheek, her gaze fixed on his terrified eyes. Ben's breath came in short, ragged puffs, his eyes wide as she leaned in, her lips parting to reveal crooked, stained teeth. She whispered something low, her words a garbled mix of grunts and laughter, her voice filled with a twisted affection that made Ben's skin crawl.

The teenage boy, the eldest child, was next to move. His face was half-hidden beneath a mess of hair and scars, his body twisted and hunched. He held a length of rusted chain in one hand, swinging it back and forth as he approached Jake, his gaze locked onto his captive's face. The boy's grin stretched wider, revealing a row of uneven, yellowed teeth, his mouth twitching with excitement.

He raised the chain, letting it dangle just inches from Jake's face, watching his eyes flicker with fear. The boy laughed, a sound that was low and guttural, filled with cruel glee. Then, without warning, he began to wrap the chain around Jake's torso, the metal biting into his flesh, cold and unforgiving.

Jake's mind screamed in pain as the chain dug deeper, the rough links pressing into his skin, but he remained silent, his body trapped, his voice swallowed by the spore's hold. The boy tightened the chain until Jake's breathing became shallow, restricted, his chest heaving with the effort of each breath.

The other children circled the fire, their movements slow and methodical, their eyes darting between the captives, their faces filled with a disturbing eagerness. The ten-year-old boy, his face marked with scars and his mouth twisted into a permanent sneer, approached Sarah, his eyes gleaming as he knelt down beside her. He ran a hand over her arm, his touch rough and clumsy, as if examining her like a piece of meat.

The little girl, the youngest, still clutching the bloodied machete, moved toward Claire. She crouched beside her, her eyes wide and unblinking, studying her face with a strange fascination. She reached out, her tiny fingers gripping a lock of Claire's hair, tugging on it with a childlike curiosity.

The father finally stepped forward, his presence commanding as he grunted a few words to his children. They looked up, their faces lighting up with excitement, and immediately moved to obey.

The eldest boy, his crooked grin widening, lifted the length of chain and raised it high above his head. He brought it down hard, the metal slamming into Jake's side with a sickening thud. Jake's body jerked, pain shooting through his ribs, but he remained silent, his screams trapped within him.

The boy raised the chain again, bringing it down in a brutal rhythm, each impact accompanied by a low grunt, a sound of satisfaction, as if he were savoring the pain he was inflicting. The others watched, their faces alight with twisted joy, each one absorbed in the spectacle, their expressions vacant but filled with a sick glee.

The mother moved to Ben, her hands reaching out to grasp his face. She pressed her fingers into his cheeks, forcing his mouth open, examining his teeth with a disturbing intensity. She muttered to herself, her voice low and garbled, a twisted lullaby as she inspected him like an animal at market.

Then, she reached into her pocket, pulling out a small, rusted blade. Without hesitation, she pressed the tip against his lip, drawing a thin line of blood. Ben's eyes widened, his mind screaming, but his body remained still, frozen in place as she continued her examination.

Satisfied, she moved back, her face twisted into a smile as she looked at the other captives, her one good eye gleaming with pride.

The little girl, still holding the severed arm she'd taken from Jake, approached Sarah, her face split into a wide grin. She lifted the limb, waving it in Sarah's face, her silent giggle a disturbing echo of innocence twisted beyond recognition.

Around the fire, the family continued their ritual, each of them taking turns with the captives, their hands and voices low and rough, their movements filled with a terrifying, deliberate cruelty. They moved with a practiced ease, each step, each gesture, a part of a dark, unspoken ritual.

The father finally let out a grunt, signaling the end of their "preparations." The family stepped back, watching their captives, their faces filled with anticipation, their bodies tense as if ready to pounce.

The clearing fell silent, the crackling of the fire the only sound, its flames casting long shadows across the snow, flickering over the twisted forms of the family as they stood over their prey.

And as the fire burned, the family looked on, their eyes glinting in the firelight, their faces alight with a hunger that would not be sated by mere flesh. They had found their prey, and they would savor every last moment of suffering.

The captives lay bound and paralyzed, their minds trapped in a nightmare from which there would be no

escape.

Chapter Six: The Matriarch's Tale

The firelight cast shadows that twisted and crawled over the trees as the family gathered around the bound, paralyzed captives. Their deformed faces gleamed with anticipation, eyes shining with a cruel, almost childish excitement. They were waiting for someone.

The clearing was filled with an oppressive silence, broken only by the crackle of the fire. Each captive lay helpless, half-buried in snow, bound and broken, unable to move, unable to scream. Only their eyes shifted, darting from face to face, desperate for a reprieve that would never come.

And then she emerged.

From the depths of the forest, dragging herself forward with great, heaving breaths, came the Matriarch.

She was a hulking mass of flesh and twisted bone, her form barely recognizable as human. Her skin was blotchy and thick, lumps and scars scattered across her body like patches of diseased earth. One eye sat lower than the other, sunken and yellow, blinking slowly as it focused on the terrified strangers lying before her. Her mouth stretched wide in a crooked, open-mouthed grin, revealing rows of blackened teeth. As she moved, her heavy, labored breaths came in wheezing gasps, filling the air with a foul, damp smell.

The family members shifted eagerly, their faces alight with cruel glee as they watched her approach. They loved this part—the story, the look of dawning horror, the moment the captives realized there was no escape, only the horrific end that awaited them.

The Matriarch stopped just a few feet from Jake, her bloated form towering over him, her breath hot and rancid. She tilted her head, her low-set eye narrowing as she studied him, her mouth stretching into a twisted grin. Then, slowly, she began to speak.

"Do you know why you're here?" she rasped, her voice a low, guttural sound that seemed to crawl over the captives like fingers tracing their skin. Her grin widened as she took in their silent, pleading faces, relishing every flicker of fear in their eyes. "Do you know why the forest brought you to us?"

The Matriarch didn't wait for an answer. Her voice slithered through the silence, cold and mocking, each word heavy with cruel satisfaction.

"This forest," she began, gesturing with one bloated, lump-ridden arm, "it has needs, you see. It's not just trees and roots—it's alive, older than any of you could imagine. It calls to people like you, pulls you in, and once you're here, there's no turning back."

Her deformed face broke into a wide, toothless grin as she watched the captives' eyes widen in horror. She knew they couldn't move, couldn't scream, but their terror was palpable. And she fed off it.

"The spores, those little things you breathed in, they're its way of holding you here, of keeping you still. A trap, you see." She chuckled, a wet, rattling sound that echoed through the clearing. "They paralyze you, make sure you can't run away. But they don't work on us. No, we're special. We've been given... immunity."

The Matriarch gestured to her family, each one twisted and grotesque, their deformed faces grinning with excitement as they looked down at their prey.

"We earned that immunity," she continued, her voice filled with a twisted pride. "Generations ago, our ancestors struck a deal with the forest. They were starving, trapped in a winter that wouldn't end, and they turned to the forest for help. They offered a sacrifice—a blood offering—and the forest accepted. It gave them the spores, taught them how to harvest them, how to make them a part of themselves."

As the Matriarch spoke, her words became a grisly tale, pulling the captives into the twisted origins of the family.

The first generation, she explained, was a group of starving settlers, isolated by a brutal winter. Their survival was hopeless; frostbite took fingers and toes, starvation hollowed their cheeks. Desperate, they turned to the forest, begging it for help, pleading with it to spare them.

In the dead of night, they performed a ritual—a ritual drenched in blood. They slaughtered the weakest among them, smearing the ground with his blood, and waited. Soon, the spores began to rise, a shimmering mist that swirled around them like a living entity.

The forest whispered to them, guiding them to ingest the spores, mix them with the blood of their fallen kin. Each person took a handful of blood-soaked spores, swallowing it in a gruesome, life-altering ceremony.

"The spores," the Matriarch said, her voice low and reverent, "bonded with their blood, changed them from the inside out. They became part of the forest—its servants, its guardians. They were no longer... human."

She laughed, a deep, raspy sound, as she gestured to her own grotesque body. "The forest gives us life, but it also demands... sacrifice. Over time, we changed. We became... closer to it."

She stretched out her arm, pointing to her low-set eye, her twisted skin. "Each generation, we changed a little more. We grew closer to the forest, became more like it. This... is the cost of loyalty. The forest keeps us alive, keeps us immune from its traps, but it marks us."

The captives' eyes widened as she spoke, the horror sinking in. They realized that these people weren't just sadistic killers—they were bound to the forest in a way that twisted both body and mind, a bond they embraced with disturbing pride.

Her grin grew wider as she watched them struggle against their bindings, each of them desperate to escape the nightmare surrounding them.

"The forest is always hungry," she continued, her voice taking on a softer, almost reverent tone. "It needs flesh, needs blood, to survive. And we are here to feed it."

She explained that every intruder was drawn in by the forest, caught by the spores, and paralyzed. "The spores," she whispered, leaning close to each captive in turn, "they trap you, keep you here for us. And when we... take from you, the spores absorb what's left. Your blood, your flesh—it goes back into the ground, into the roots, into the trees."

Her family members nodded eagerly, their twisted faces alight with savage delight. Each one moved closer, their deformed limbs bending awkwardly as they leaned in to watch, to savor the fear in the captives' eyes.

"This is how we keep the forest alive. This is why it gives us immunity. We bring it what it needs, and in return... it keeps us safe."

The Matriarch moved around the fire, stopping beside each captive, her bloated, deformed hand trailing over their faces. Her touch was cold, her skin rough and clammy.

"Outsiders like you," she sneered, "you're just... food. You're nothing but sustenance. Trespassers in our land, brought here to serve the forest's needs. You see, we don't view this as cruelty." She chuckled, the sound thick and mocking. "No, to us, this is divine."

The family members grinned, their mouths twitching as they watched their matriarch speak. They knew the ritual, the story by heart, and they waited with eager anticipation for the part they loved most—the realization, the horror that dawned on each captive as they grasped the truth.

The Matriarch leaned close, her foul breath washing over Sarah's face. "You'll be here forever," she whispered. "Your bones will stay here, just like all the others. And we'll keep feeding the forest, keep honoring it, long after you're gone."

The Matriarch's story shifted to another memory, her voice filling the clearing with echoes of horror. She recounted the first ritual of sacrifice performed by her ancestors, a rite drenched in blood and terror.

In the dark of night, they gathered around their prey, each person playing their part as they carved the intruders, feeding the forest with flesh and bone. They were guided by whispers, voices that drifted through the trees, instructing them on how to honor the spores, how to ensure the forest's survival.

The family's ancestors had relished each kill, taking pride in the forest's approval. They could feel it in the ground, in the trees, a pulse of satisfaction, a dark, primal hunger that they had learned to feed.

The Matriarch returned to the present, her eye gleaming as she looked over the bound captives, each one stricken with terror. She leaned in, her mouth close to Jake's ear, her voice a cold, mocking whisper.

"My family likes to watch," the Matriarch whispered, her grin spreading even wider, a grotesque display of cracked, blackened teeth. "They love the fear, love the look in your eyes when you realize exactly what's going to happen to you. The helplessness. The horror."

She turned to the family, each member's twisted face lit up with sick anticipation, eyes gleaming in the firelight. They were barely human now, closer to animals, feeding off the terror they'd cultivated in their captives.

"But the best part?" The Matriarch's voice dropped lower, her tone almost tender, mocking. "It's when you understand... that you're not just going to die. No, you're going to die in pieces, watching yourself disappear, bit by bit."

She lumbered over to Claire, running her lumpy, mottled hand over her hair. Claire's body remained still, trapped in place, but her eyes were wild with terror, every inch of her screaming silently. The Matriarch's heavy fingers traced down Claire's cheek, her touch slow and deliberate.

"See, my children... they have their own way of honoring the forest," she said, her gaze moving to the youngest child, the little girl still holding Jake's severed arm like a prize. "They're hungry, you see. Hungry and eager. And you, my dears... well, you're tonight's feast."

The little girl's face twisted into a wide, unnatural grin as she lifted the arm, waving it in front of Claire, letting blood drip onto the snow. The family watched, transfixed, their faces lit with savage glee.

The Matriarch's rasping voice filled the clearing, carrying the final, horrifying revelation. "Each of you will watch as they take you apart, piece by piece, until there's nothing left but bones for the forest to feed on. You're not just here to die—you're here to satisfy its hunger, to become part of its life."

She straightened, her heavy, hulking form casting a monstrous shadow over the captives. "So scream, if you can. I'd love to hear it."

And as the fire crackled and the family gathered around, ready to begin their twisted feast, the Matriarch leaned back, her laughter—a hollow, guttural sound—echoing through the forest, mingling with the silent screams of her captives, who knew now, with horrifying certainty, that there would be no escape.

Chapter Seven: Feast of Horrors

The world was silent. Cold, dark, and silent.

One by one, the captives stirred. Awareness crept in slowly, dragging them from the depths of unconsciousness, each sense tingling back to life. Their bodies ached, limbs frozen in place by the unyielding grip of the spores. But as their vision cleared, as the cold faded into the background, a new sensation hit them—a sound. A wet, repetitive hacking, heavy and sickening, filled the clearing, slicing through the quiet like a cruel taunt.

Sarah's mind fought through the haze. Her eyes blinked open, fixed on the dim glow of the fire nearby, but her body remained locked, her muscles paralyzed, her breaths short and sharp. She tried to turn her head, but nothing responded. All she could do was listen.

Hack. Hack.

The sound was thick, brutal, each swing landing with a wet, sickening squelch. And then the smell hit her—the unmistakable, nauseating scent of burning flesh.

Her mind screamed in recognition, a primal horror that took her breath away. It was Jake. They were... hacking him apart.

Her eyes darted wildly, searching for her friends, each of them bound and paralyzed around the clearing, their expressions frozen in horror as they watched the nightmare unfold.

Around the fire, the family had gathered, their deformed faces lit by the flames, twisted in expressions of glee and hunger. The father stood over Jake's body, one massive, gnarled hand gripping a cleaver, his movements calm and methodical as he hacked into Jake's limbs, separating flesh from bone.

Beside him, the teenage son grinned, his misshapen face contorting as he watched each piece fall. His scarred hands reached eagerly for the meat, tossing chunks onto a rusted, blackened grill set up above the fire. The flesh sizzled and popped, a grisly aroma filling the air, mingling with the scent of the earth and snow. It was sickening, invasive, each breath tainted by the metallic tang of cooked blood.

The youngest, the little girl, stood clutching Jake's severed arm, swinging it like a toy, her face split in a gleeful grin as she watched the fire. Her movements were jerky, animalistic, her eyes fixed on the captives as if daring them to look away.

Claire's vision blurred with tears, her body screaming to flee, to move, to do anything but watch. But she was helpless, her muscles locked in place, the spores holding her captive as she witnessed the desecration of her friend.

Suddenly, the little girl turned, her small, twisted face lighting up with a new idea. She dropped Jake's arm, her hands reaching for his severed head, gripping it by the hair. The lifeless eyes stared blankly as she lifted it, her expression one of pure, childlike glee.

With a twisted laugh, she skipped over to the bound captives, holding Jake's head inches from their faces, forcing each one to confront the lifeless gaze of their friend.

She pressed Jake's face close to Sarah's, the cold, bloody skin brushing against her cheek. Sarah's eyes filled with tears, her mind reeling as the child pulled the head back, making Jake's mouth "speak" in a mocking, garbled voice.

"Look, he's saying goodbye," the girl taunted, her tone filled with cruel mirth. She giggled, moving to each captive in turn, making Jake's head "talk" to each one. The family laughed, clapping and cheering her on as she continued her sick game.

Ben's body shook, his mind drowning in horror as the little girl leaned in, holding Jake's head close, her eyes shining with twisted amusement. She tilted Jake's face, making him look straight into Ben's eyes, the dead gaze unseeing but hauntingly real.

The family roared with laughter, their deformed faces alight with savage joy as they watched the captives' expressions contort in horror and despair.

The mother, her face skeletal and sunken, shuffled toward the fire. Her bony hands reached out, grabbing a piece of Jake's cooked flesh from the grill. She held it up, examining it with a twisted smile before she turned to the captives.

With a grin, she moved to Claire, her eyes gleaming with sadistic intent. She reached down, prying Claire's mouth open, and shoved the piece of flesh inside, her fingers forcing it between her lips.

Claire's eyes widened in horror as the taste hit her—a mixture of charred fat and blood, a flavor so vile it threatened to choke her. She tried to gag, to spit it out, but the mother clamped her hand over Claire's mouth, forcing her to swallow.

The family laughed, clapping and cheering as Claire's body convulsed, her face twisted in revulsion. The mother moved on, repeating the ritual with each captive, ensuring that each one "shared" in the meal.

Sarah's vision blurred with tears as the mother forced a piece of Jake's flesh into her mouth, the greasy meat sticking to her tongue, filling her senses with the taste of death. She wanted to scream, to thrash, to run, but her body remained paralyzed, trapped in the nightmare that surrounded her.

The family watched with gleeful anticipation, their laughter echoing through the clearing as they reveled in the captives' helplessness.

The teenage son, his face twisted in a mocking grin, grabbed one of Jake's arms, lifting it like a puppet. He bent the fingers, making it "wave" at the captives, his laughter low and guttural as he taunted them with the lifeless limb.

He dragged the arm across the snow, leaving a trail of blood, before lifting it and slapping Ben's face with it, laughing harder as he repeated the cruel gesture. Ben's face contorted in horror, his eyes wide with terror, but he was powerless to stop it, forced to endure the sick game.

The little girl, still holding Jake's head, continued her twisted performance, making it "speak" to each captive, her voice high and mocking. She moved from one to the next, delighting in their horror, her laughter blending with the crackling of the fire as she brought Jake's face inches from their own.

The Matriarch stood nearby, her bloated, deformed form casting a monstrous shadow over the clearing. She watched her family's twisted rituals with a satisfied grin, her eyes gleaming with dark pride.

"This is our way," she intoned, her voice thick and mocking. "The forest demands sacrifice, and we are happy to provide."

She moved closer to the captives, her heavy footsteps crunching in the snow. Her face hovered inches from Sarah's, her breath hot and foul as she continued.

"Each piece of him you swallow, each taste of flesh, brings you closer to the forest. Soon, you will join him, each of you, in pieces, just like he did."

She turned to her children, her voice rising in a chant, her words a twisted mockery of reverence as she urged them on. The family followed, each member gripping a piece of Jake's flesh, lifting it high as they began a slow, rhythmic dance around the fire.

The captives watched in helpless horror as the family moved in a circle, chanting, grunting, their bodies swaying in a savage, primal dance. Each of them held a piece of Jake, lifting it high with each step, their laughter mingling with the crackling of the flames.

The father, his face twisted in a grotesque smile, approached each captive, holding up a piece of Jake's flesh, taunting them with the sight and smell of it.

He pressed the meat close to Ben's face, his voice a low, mocking whisper. "This is what waits for you. This is the honor you'll receive."

He moved to each captive, repeating the ritual, each word dripping with cruelty as he promised them the same fate, piece by piece, until there was nothing left but bones for the forest to claim.

The little girl, still clutching Jake's head, brought it close to each captive, holding it inches from their faces, the dead eyes staring into theirs with hollow finality.

As the night wore on, the family continued their grotesque ritual, their laughter and chanting filling the clearing, their voices merging into a cacophony of horror. The fire burned low, the smell of charred flesh hanging heavy in the air, each breath filled with the taste of death.

The captives lay bound and paralyzed, their bodies numb, their minds shattered by the horror they had witnessed. Each one lay in silent despair, their hearts pounding, their thoughts filled with the knowledge of their fate.

The Matriarch stood over them, her face split into a wide, twisted grin as she watched them suffer. She leaned close, her voice a low, mocking whisper.

"This is just the beginning," she promised. "Soon, each of you will join him. Piece by piece."

And as the fire crackled and the embers glowed in the dim light, the family's twisted ritual dragged on, a nightmarish display of cruelty and deranged devotion. The captives lay silent, their minds screaming beneath the paralyzing hold of the spores, forced to witness the slow dismantling of their friend, the horror of what awaited each of them etched into their minds with brutal clarity.

The Matriarch stood over them, her shadow looming as she took her place by the dying fire. Her family moved in chaotic reverence around her, their laughter echoing through the trees, each twisted face alight with a savage joy. She watched, savoring every flicker of terror in the captives' wide eyes, every shudder of revulsion that passed over their faces.

At last, the night deepened, and the family's macabre revelry slowed. The children yawned, their eyes heavy with satisfaction as they sank down into the snow beside the fire, each clutching a remnant of their feast. The mother and father gathered close, casting one last satisfied glance at the bound captives before settling into the snow, huddling together like a grotesque tableau of innocence shattered beyond recognition.

The Matriarch's heavy, wheezing breaths filled the quiet, her gaze moving from one captive to the next. She leaned over them, her voice a low, rasping whisper.

"Sleep now," she murmured, her grin splitting her bloated face. "Rest while you can. Tomorrow... tomorrow, the forest will take what it's owed."

She reached out, her cold, heavy fingers trailing over Sarah's face, her touch lingering like a final curse.

And as the fire sputtered, casting shadows that danced and flickered over the twisted faces of the family, the clearing fell into an eerie silence. The captives lay in the snow, their bodies locked in horror, their minds filled with the relentless knowledge of what awaited them with the next dawn.

The family would feed again, and each of them would meet the same grisly fate as Jake, piece by bloody piece.

With the clearing blanketed in darkness, the forest stood watch over the grotesque scene, its ancient hunger temporarily sated, waiting for the next ritual, the next sacrifice. And in the silence, the captives lay helpless, knowing that the nightmare was only just beginning.

Chapter Eight: Desperation and Defiance

The clearing was still. Dawn crept through the trees, casting long shadows over the forest floor. Each breath hung in the air, visible in the cold, misting around the captives, who lay scattered, bound and half-buried in snow, surrounded by the silent, twisted figures of the family.

Sarah's mind emerged slowly from unconsciousness, each sensation coming back one by one. The taste of blood in her mouth. The rough bindings biting into her wrists. The icy numbness spreading through her legs, buried beneath layers of snow. And then—the faintest flicker of feeling in her fingers.

She wasn't entirely paralyzed. She could feel it, that tiny hint of movement. Her fingers twitched, just barely, but it was something.

Heart pounding, Sarah focused all her energy on her hand, willing it to move. She strained, teeth clenched, feeling the slightest response from her arm. She glanced over at the others, desperately hoping they'd noticed. Across the clearing, she locked eyes with Claire, whose face was pale and wide-eyed with fear. But as Claire shifted slightly, a spark of hope ignited in Sarah's chest. Claire had felt it too.

Next to Claire, Ben lay still, his gaze fixed on the gray sky above, his breaths shallow and visible in the chill air. Sarah's gaze flicked from him to Claire, their eyes communicating everything they couldn't say aloud. They all knew—this might be their only chance.

The morning light cast everything in a gray, lifeless haze. It was deathly silent, the only sounds the soft crackling of the fire's last embers and the slow, steady breaths of the family around them. They lay sprawled around the clearing, their deformed forms twisted in slumber, some curled in fetal positions, others spread out like marionettes with severed strings.

Sarah's gaze shifted to the hulking figure of the Matriarch, her bloated, twisted form hunched in the shadows. Her face was contorted in sleep, her mouth hanging open, revealing blackened teeth. Her chest rose and fell slowly, her breaths rattling, a faint wheeze breaking the silence.

With the family asleep, Sarah felt the flicker of hope grow. She strained against her bindings, willing her arm to move, her fingers to clench. Every second counted, each heartbeat pounding louder in her ears as she fought against the paralyzing effects of the spores.

Ben's eyes darted to her, his face filled with a desperate, silent plea. He, too, was struggling, his hands twitching, his legs shifting beneath the snow. Claire's lips were pressed tightly together, her expression a mixture of terror and determination as she fought against the invisible chains holding her body captive.

Each of them was awakening, feeling their muscles respond, their bodies reclaiming small measures of control. And each knew they had to act fast—the family would awaken soon, and their chances of escape would be gone.

The quiet was shattered by a low, wheezing groan. Sarah's eyes snapped to the Matriarch, whose eyes had opened, fixing on the captives with a slow, deliberate gaze. Her twisted, misshapen face split into a grin as she pushed herself up, her heavy, bloated form moving with surprising grace.

She said nothing, only watched them, her gaze lingering on each captive in turn, taking in every detail—their pale faces, the faint movement of their limbs. A flicker of amusement crossed her features as she noticed the captives' struggles, the faint traces of movement in their hands and legs.

One by one, the rest of the family stirred, their twisted faces breaking into sleepy, eager grins as they realized what lay before them. The father sat up, his eyes gleaming as he spotted Sarah's slight movements, his face splitting into a hungry smile.

The teenage son, with his crooked spine and gleaming, vacant eyes, let out a low chuckle, his hands twitching eagerly. He grabbed a length of chain, swinging it back and forth as he watched them, his gaze flicking between Sarah, Claire, and Ben, as though deciding which one to drag forward first.

The youngest, the little girl, still clutched Jake's severed arm, her fingers wrapped around it like a prized possession. She giggled, her face filled with innocent delight as she noticed the captives' eyes darting back and forth, taking in their surroundings, their bodies straining against their bonds.

The family gathered around the fire, their faces lit by the dim light, their twisted expressions filled with hunger and anticipation. They remained silent, each one's gaze fixed on the captives, their eyes cold and calculating. There was no need for words; the message was clear. The captives' time was running out.

The Matriarch moved slowly around the clearing, her gaze never leaving the captives. She leaned over Ben, her breath hot and foul against his face as she whispered, "The forest has chosen you. It's hungry."

Her words were barely a whisper, but they carried a weight that filled the clearing, pressing down on the captives like a heavy fog. She moved to Claire, her bony fingers trailing over her face, her touch cold and clammy. "Today, you become part of something… greater."

The family watched, their eyes gleaming with excitement as the Matriarch moved from one captive to the next, her presence a chilling reminder of what awaited them. She didn't need to explain further; her gaze, her touch, was enough to convey the horror of their fate.

The captives were helpless, bound and immobile, forced to endure the Matriarch's taunts, her cold fingers tracing lines over their faces, her words filling their minds with a deep, consuming dread.

As the family gathered around the fire, Sarah focused on the small amount of movement she'd regained. She strained against her bindings, her fingers twitching, her wrists shifting against the ropes. Her mind raced, each second ticking away as she calculated her next move.

She glanced at Claire, who nodded almost imperceptibly, her face set in determination. Ben's gaze met hers, his expression filled with a mixture of fear and resolve. They each knew what was at stake; this might be their only chance.

With her fingers curled around the edge of her bindings, Sarah felt the ropes begin to loosen, inch by inch. Her heart pounded, her breaths coming in short, quiet gasps as she worked, each movement small but purposeful.

Across from her, Claire struggled with her own bindings, her movements slow and careful. The family's eyes were on the fire,

COLD CUTS

their attention momentarily distracted, their faces filled with anticipation for the "feast" to come.

But just as Sarah felt the ropes loosen enough for her to free her hand, the Matriarch's gaze snapped to her, a flicker of suspicion in her cold, calculating eyes.

Sarah froze, her heart pounding, her body tensing as the Matriarch approached. The Matriarch's eyes narrowed, her twisted grin widening as she leaned close.

Her face loomed inches from Sarah's, her breath hot and foul. She tilted her head, watching Sarah's fingers twitch, her grin widening as she realized what Sarah was trying to do.

With a slow, mocking smile, the Matriarch reached down, her fingers wrapping around Sarah's wrist, tightening the bindings with deliberate force. Sarah's face twisted in pain, her hope fading as the Matriarch's grip held her fast.

But as the Matriarch moved on, her gaze turning to Ben, Sarah felt a surge of defiance. She couldn't stay silent, couldn't let them win without a fight. With the last bit of strength she could muster, she lashed out, her fist connecting weakly with the teenage son's deformed face.

The blow was weak, her muscles still sluggish from the spores, but it was enough to catch him off guard. He stumbled back, his face twisted in shock and anger as he recovered, his gaze narrowing with fury.

The family erupted in laughter, their twisted faces alight with amusement as they watched Sarah's defiance, savoring the brief moment of rebellion before closing in around her, tightening her bindings even further.

The Matriarch let out a low chuckle, her eyes filled with cruel satisfaction as she leaned close. "Fighting back, are we? It won't save you," she whispered, her voice a mocking taunt that filled Sarah's mind with dread.

With Sarah's bindings tightened, the family settled into a chilling silence, their eyes fixed on the captives, each face filled with anticipation. The Matriarch's gaze moved over each one, lingering on Ben, her expression filled with a twisted sense of reverence.

The family began to chant in low, guttural voices, their words blending together in a haunting melody that filled the clearing. The sound was slow and rhythmic, each note resonating through the forest, wrapping around the captives like a dark, oppressive fog.

Sarah felt the weight of their fate pressing down on her, the finality of it sinking in as the family's voices grew louder, filling the air with a sense of inevitable doom.

They were trapped, helpless, caught in the forest's grip, surrounded by a family that saw them as nothing more than prey.

And as the morning sun rose, casting a pale light over the clearing, Sarah, Claire, and Ben braced themselves for the horror that awaited them, each one clinging to the last shreds of hope as the family prepared for the feast.

Chapter Nine: The Matriarch's Final Feast

THE FAMILY'S LOW, RHYTHMIC chant filled the clearing, each note reverberating through the frozen air. Sarah's heart pounded as she struggled against her bindings, her fingers trembling as she tried to keep her movement hidden. The Matriarch stood at the center, her deformed face illuminated by the flickering flames of the fire, her eyes gleaming with a twisted, triumphant light.

Around her, the family members gathered, each one grinning with dark excitement as they prepared for the ritual. The teenage son swung his chain in slow arcs, his crooked grin fixed on Ben, whose face had drained of color. The father gripped a jagged, rusted knife in one hand, his expression one of grim satisfaction.

Ben's body trembled as he realized he'd been chosen. His eyes darted to Sarah and Claire, desperation and fear clouding his gaze as the family closed in around him.

With a grunt, the father grabbed Ben by the arm, dragging him roughly toward the fire. Ben struggled, his movements sluggish, his strength fading as the spores' effects lingered. The teenage son moved beside him, binding his wrists with a thick chain, tightening it until Ben's arms were pinned behind his back, his body forced to kneel by the flames.

The Matriarch stepped forward, her hands raised as if in prayer, her gaze fixed on Ben with a cold, mocking reverence.

"You are the forest's gift," she intoned, her voice thick with dark satisfaction. "Your blood will nourish the soil, your flesh will feed its roots. Today, you become part of something... greater."

Ben's face contorted in horror, his mouth opening in a silent scream as he struggled against his bindings. But his efforts were futile; the father's grip was unyielding, his expression merciless as he prepared to carry out the Matriarch's commands.

The teenage son handed the father the jagged knife, his face filled with eager anticipation as he watched, his twisted features illuminated by the firelight.

The father lifted the blade, its edge glinting in the dim light as he placed it against Ben's shoulder. He pressed down slowly, slicing through the skin with brutal, deliberate force. Ben's body convulsed, his face twisted in agony as the blade bit deeper, cutting through muscle and sinew, each movement sending waves of pain through his body.

The family watched, their faces alight with savage glee as they took in every flicker of pain, every silent scream that crossed Ben's face. The little girl clutched Jake's severed head, her eyes wide with delight as she leaned close, watching Ben's suffering with the innocent curiosity of a child.

The father carved away a chunk of flesh, holding it up as blood dripped from the blade, staining the snow. He turned to the Matriarch, offering the piece with a solemn nod.

The Matriarch accepted it, her face splitting into a wide, grotesque grin as she held the flesh up to the sky. "The forest accepts this offering," she murmured, her voice filled with a sick, reverent joy. She bit into the flesh, tearing away a piece with her blackened teeth, her gaze fixed on the captives as she chewed, her expression one of twisted satisfaction.

One by one, each family member took their own piece, biting into the raw flesh, their faces smeared with blood as they consumed their grisly meal. The youngest child took her piece with eager hands, clutching it as though it were a prized treat, her face alight with glee as she devoured it.

Sarah and Claire watched in horror, their bodies frozen in place, their minds reeling as they witnessed the brutal desecration of their friend. Every instinct screamed at them to look away, to close their eyes, but they couldn't—they were trapped, forced to endure every agonizing second.

As the family finished their meal, the Matriarch turned her gaze to Sarah and Claire, her eyes gleaming with cruel amusement. She moved toward them, her heavy, bloated form casting a shadow over their paralyzed bodies, her grin widening as she saw the terror in their eyes.

"You'll join him soon," she whispered, her voice low and mocking. "Each of you will serve the forest, just as he has."

She reached down, her cold, clammy fingers trailing over Sarah's face, her touch sending shivers down her spine. Sarah clenched her fists, her fingers curling into tight balls as she struggled against the fear, her mind racing with desperate plans for escape.

The Matriarch moved to Claire, her fingers gripping her chin, forcing her to look up. "The forest will remember you," she murmured, her breath hot and foul against Claire's face. "Your bones will remain, your blood will feed its roots. You are... honored."

Claire's eyes filled with tears, her body trembling as the Matriarch's words sank in, the finality of her fate weighing down on her like a crushing force.

As the Matriarch moved back toward the fire, Sarah focused all her energy on the slight movement she'd regained. She could feel the ropes loosening, her wrists shifting against the bindings as she strained, her fingers curling around the edges.

With a final, desperate effort, Sarah managed to free one hand. Her heart raced as she quietly worked at the ropes binding her legs, her eyes fixed on the family, hoping they wouldn't notice.

But just as she freed her second hand, her foot brushed against a branch, the sound echoing through the clearing like a gunshot.

The Matriarch's head snapped toward her, her eyes narrowing with fury. The family turned in unison, their faces twisted with rage as they realized what she was attempting.

The teenage son lunged forward, his chain swinging, his face filled with anger as he grabbed her, his fingers digging into her skin as he forced her back to the ground. Sarah struggled, her body thrashing as she fought against his grip, but the family was too strong, their hold unyielding.

The Matriarch let out a low, mocking laugh, her eyes filled with dark satisfaction as she watched Sarah's failed escape. "Did you really think you could get away?" she taunted, her voice filled with cold amusement. "The forest has already claimed you."

The father returned to Ben, his expression cold and focused as he resumed his brutal work. Ben's face was pale, his body trembling as he endured each slice, each cut, his mind slipping into a haze of agony and despair.

The family continued their feast, each member taking turns as they carved pieces from Ben, treating each one like a sacred offering, a tribute to the forest's insatiable hunger.

Sarah watched, her heart breaking as Ben's body slumped, his breaths coming in short, shallow gasps as he struggled to hold on. She wanted to scream, to fight, to do something—anything—to save him, but she was helpless, trapped, forced to watch as her friend was slowly consumed.

As Ben's life slipped away, the family fell silent, their faces alight with satisfaction as they gathered around his body, their hands and faces smeared with blood.

The Matriarch raised her hands, her voice a low, guttural chant that echoed through the clearing, filling the forest with a haunting, reverent silence. The family joined in, their voices blending together in a chilling harmony, each note resonating with a sense of dark finality.

They had completed the ritual, their offering accepted, their hunger satisfied.

As the family's voices faded, Sarah felt a surge of determination. Ben's sacrifice wouldn't be in vain. She focused on her bindings, her fingers working at the ropes, her movements slow and careful as she plotted her next move.

The family's attention was elsewhere, their faces filled with dark satisfaction as they prepared to move on to the next victim.

But Sarah knew that, somehow, she had to escape. She had to survive—for herself, for Claire, Jake and for Ben.

Chapter Ten: One Last Desperate Look

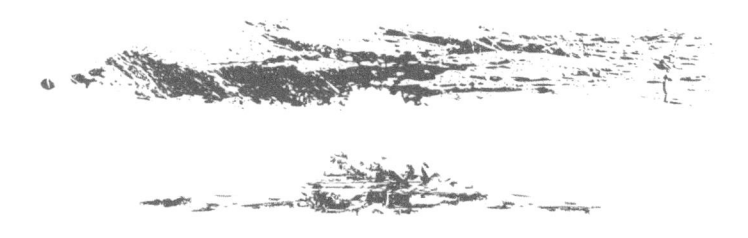

THE AIR WAS DENSE AND sharp as Sarah and Claire sat in silence, bound and broken in the clearing. Ben's brutal death lingered in their minds, casting a suffocating shadow over them. Every breath felt heavy, each heartbeat an echo of horror. Sarah blinked slowly, the cold cutting through her skin, her numb fingers starting to tingle as feeling returned. Beside her, Claire was shivering, her face pale as a ghost.

"Sarah..." Claire's voice was barely a whisper, a terrified sound that vanished into the quiet. Sarah turned her head, meeting Claire's gaze, the raw fear in her eyes enough to shatter any hope. But Sarah held steady.

"We're getting out of here," Sarah whispered back, her voice steady despite the tremor in her hands. "Hold on. Just... hold on."

She shifted her wrists, feeling the rough bite of the ropes around her skin. Every movement sent a sharp sting through her hands, but she gritted her teeth, focusing on loosening her bonds. Each twist, every flex, brought her closer to freedom. Sarah kept her eyes on Claire, her expression fierce, a quiet fire burning behind her gaze.

"Focus on getting free," she muttered, each word laced with a desperation she couldn't afford to show. "We're getting out. Together."

The ropes bit into her skin, each fiber scraping her wrists as she worked her fingers under the knots, tugging and pulling, inch by inch. Time slowed, every second stretching out painfully, her heartbeat thundering in her ears. Her body ached from the spores' effects, the cold, and the weight of the night's horror, but she didn't stop.

Claire was doing the same, her movements quiet, each shift careful to avoid drawing attention. The family slept soundly around the clearing, their twisted, deformed bodies sprawled in grotesque positions. The little girl still clutched Jake's severed arm, her fingers sticky with dried blood, her face twisted in a sick, contented smile.

Sarah's breath hitched as she felt the rope around her wrists loosen, the fibers beginning to give way. She shot a glance at Claire, who nodded, a hint of hope lighting her eyes.

"Almost... there..." Sarah muttered, gritting her teeth as she worked the rope down her wrists. Finally, the last knot slipped, and her hands were free.

Sarah quickly moved to untie her legs, her fingers working quickly as her eyes darted around the clearing. She motioned to Claire, who was watching her with wide eyes, and began untying her friend's bindings, each motion slow and deliberate. The firelight flickered, casting shadows that danced across the clearing, distorting the family's slumbering forms into monstrous shapes.

Once Claire was free, they exchanged a tense glance, their unspoken understanding solidifying. Without a word, they rose to their feet, their movements careful as they slipped away from the clearing, leaving behind the grotesque figures of their captors.

They moved through the trees, the snow crunching softly beneath their feet, each step calculated to avoid making noise. The forest loomed around them, dark and dense, the trees twisted and gnarled, their branches reaching down like skeletal hands.

As they ventured deeper, a strange sensation began to settle over them. The air grew thick, heavy, the smell of decay mingling with the cold bite of the snow. The forest felt alive, each shadow watching them, each branch seeming to pulse with a dark, malevolent energy.

"Sarah..." Claire whispered, her voice trembling. "Something's wrong. I can feel it... in my bones."

Sarah shushed her, gripping her hand tightly. "Keep moving. Don't think about it."

But she felt it too—the spores' effects creeping back in, her muscles growing heavier, her breath becoming labored. She forced herself forward, each step a battle against the forest itself, her every instinct screaming that the trees were closing in around them, trapping them.

Back in the clearing, a low, guttural growl broke the silence. The Matriarch's eyes snapped open, her face twisting into a grin as she realized what had happened.

"They're gone," she hissed, her voice a rasp that sent a chill through the clearing. She rose, her heavy form casting a shadow over her slumbering family. One by one, they awoke, their twisted faces contorting in anger and excitement as they realized the captives had escaped.

The Matriarch let out a shrill cry, her voice echoing through the trees, a signal that carried through the forest like a death knell. "Find them!" she commanded, her voice laced with fury. "The forest demands them!"

The family scattered, their laughter and taunts filling the forest, blending with the wind, becoming part of the very air around them.

Sarah and Claire froze as the voices reached them, chilling them to the bone. They were close, far closer than they'd realized. Sarah tightened her grip on Claire's hand, pulling her forward as they broke into a run, their breaths coming in short, ragged gasps.

Branches clawed at their faces, snow crunching loudly beneath their feet as they stumbled through the trees, each step echoing with the sound of pursuit. The family's laughter grew louder, their voices mocking, taunting, calling out Sarah and Claire's names as though they were merely playing a game.

"Sarah!" The Matriarch's voice carried through the trees, sharp and menacing. "Come back, child. The forest has chosen you!"

The spores thickened, swirling around them in clouds, filling their lungs with each breath, their limbs growing heavier with every step. Visions flickered at the edges of their vision—ghostly faces, twisted and hollow-eyed, their mouths open in silent screams.

They stumbled into a small clearing, where ancient symbols were carved into the trees, moss-covered totems standing guard in a circle around them. The forest seemed to close in, the air thick with the scent of decay, the trees pressing down upon them like silent sentinels.

"We have to keep moving," Sarah muttered, her voice barely audible. Her vision blurred, the edges darkening as the forest's curse seeped into her mind, her thoughts clouding with fear and exhaustion.

Claire clung to Sarah, her face pale, her eyes wide with terror. "Sarah, I... I can't keep going," she whispered, her voice filled with defeat. "They're going to find us. They're going to kill us."

"No," Sarah said fiercely, gripping Claire's shoulders. "You're getting out of here. Do you hear me? You're going to live."

The sound of footsteps approached, loud and relentless, the family drawing closer with each passing second. Sarah's mind raced, each heartbeat pounding in her ears as she calculated their options.

Suddenly, the teenage son stepped into view, his chain swinging in his hand, his face twisted into a cruel grin. He blocked their path, his eyes gleaming with malice as he took a step forward, the chain clinking softly as it dragged along the ground.

"Nowhere left to run," he taunted, his voice low and mocking.

Sarah glanced at the ground, her gaze settling on a thick branch half-buried in the snow. She gripped it, feeling the rough bark dig into her palm, her fingers trembling as she raised it like a weapon.

"Claire," she whispered, her voice filled with urgency. "Run. Don't look back."

Claire hesitated, her face filled with fear and confusion. "Sarah, no—"

"Go!" Sarah shouted, her voice fierce and unyielding. "I'll catch up. Just run!"

Claire took one last, desperate look at Sarah, her eyes filled with tears, before she turned and bolted into the trees, her figure disappearing into the darkness.

Sarah turned back to the teenage son, her grip tightening on the branch, her every nerve on edge. He laughed, a low, guttural sound that echoed through the forest, his eyes alight with excitement.

"You really think you can take me?" he sneered, swinging his chain in a lazy arc.

Sarah didn't respond. She lunged forward, swinging the branch with all her strength, catching him off guard. The branch connected with his shoulder, the impact sending him stumbling back, his face twisting in rage.

He recovered quickly, his grip on the chain tightening as he advanced on her, his movements slow and menacing. Sarah ducked as he swung, the chain missing her by inches as she retaliated with another swing of the branch, her every movement fueled by desperation.

Just as Sarah felt her strength waning, the Matriarch stepped into the clearing, her hulking form looming over them, her face split into a cruel smile.

"Well done, Sarah," she taunted, clapping slowly. "Such spirit. Such defiance."

Sarah's chest heaved with exhaustion, as she locked eyes with the Matriarch, her heart pounding, her breaths shallow. The Matriarch's smile widened, her blackened teeth gleaming in the dim light. She tilted her head, watching Sarah with a mixture of amusement and hunger, as if savoring the final moments before the kill.

Sarah tightened her grip on the branch, her muscles screaming in protest, her entire body trembling with exhaustion. She knew she couldn't last much longer, but she wasn't going to go down without a fight. She took a step back, trying to put some distance between herself and the advancing Matriarch.

The teenage son regained his footing, his face twisted in fury. He lunged at Sarah, swinging the chain wildly. She dodged, barely, the chain grazing her arm and sending a sharp sting of pain through her body. She stumbled but managed to stay on her feet, her vision blurring from the impact.

"Enough of this," the Matriarch hissed, her voice low and venomous. "You're wasting our time, girl. The forest demands sacrifice, and you... you're just prolonging the inevitable."

Sarah steadied herself, her gaze hardening as she looked at the Matriarch. "I won't let you have her," she spat, defiance burning in her eyes.

The Matriarch's smile faded, replaced by a look of cold fury. She gestured to her son, who moved toward Sarah with renewed determination, his grip on the chain tightening as he prepared to strike.

But Sarah acted first. Summoning the last of her strength, she lunged forward, swinging the branch with every ounce of energy she had left. The branch struck the teenage son across the face, the impact snapping his head to the side, a spray of blood splattering across the snow.

He staggered, clutching his face, his eyes wide with shock and pain. The Matriarch let out a furious scream, her twisted face contorting with rage as she advanced on Sarah, her heavy footsteps crushing the snow beneath her.

Before Sarah could react, the Matriarch's hand shot out, grabbing her by the throat and lifting her off the ground. Sarah gasped, her fingers clawing at the Matriarch's grip as she struggled for air, her vision darkening around the edges.

"You think you can fight me?" the Matriarch sneered, her voice dripping with contempt. "You're nothing, girl. Just another offering to the forest."

Sarah's body went limp, her strength finally giving out as the Matriarch tightened her grip, her fingers digging into Sarah's skin. Spots danced before her eyes, her lungs burning as she struggled to draw breath. She felt the life draining from her, the weight of despair settling over her like a shroud.

But just before the darkness claimed her, she managed one last act of defiance. With the last ounce of her strength, Sarah spit in the Matriarch's face, her expression one of pure, unbroken defiance.

The Matriarch's face twisted in disgust and fury, but a glint of respect flickered in her eyes. She tightened her grip one last time before tossing Sarah to the ground like a rag doll, her body hitting the snow with a dull thud.

Sarah lay there, her vision swimming, her body broken and battered. She could hear the Matriarch's footsteps retreating, the family's laughter echoing through the forest as they moved away, their attention shifting to the chase for Claire.

With her last remaining strength, Sarah lifted her head, watching as the figures disappeared into the darkness, leaving her alone in the clearing. She let out a weak, shuddering breath, a faint smile crossing her lips.

She had done it. She had bought Claire time. She had given her friend a chance.

As the cold seeped into her bones, Sarah let her eyes drift shut, her mind filled with the faint hope that, somewhere out there, Claire was still running, still fighting, still alive.

The forest grew quiet around her, the shadows closing in, the snow falling softly, covering her broken body in a blanket of white. And in the silence, the forest seemed to breathe, a dark, endless hunger that would never be satisfied.

Chapter Eleven: A Leap of Faith

THE FOREST SWALLOWED Claire whole as she ran, her feet pounding through the snow, her breaths short and ragged. Every muscle in her body ached, her limbs growing heavier with each step, as though the trees themselves were reaching out to hold her back. She could still feel Sarah's presence with her, that last, fierce look before she'd turned back to face the family, buying Claire precious time to escape. The image burned into Claire's mind, a haunting reminder of everything she was leaving behind.

But there was no time to grieve. The forest loomed around her, thick with shadows and the echo of laughter drifting through the trees. The family was close—too close. She could hear their voices, calling out her name, taunting her, each sound slicing through the air like a blade.

"Run, little mouse," the Matriarch's voice echoed, smooth and mocking. "You can't escape the forest. It's already swallowed you."

Claire choked back a sob, forcing herself to keep moving, each step fueled by sheer desperation. She clung to the hope that Sarah's sacrifice hadn't been in vain, that somehow, she'd find a way out of this nightmare. Her chest burned with each breath, the cold air slicing through her lungs, but she didn't stop. She couldn't.

As Claire stumbled deeper into the forest, a strange sensation settled over her. The trees seemed to shift, twisting in impossible shapes, their branches stretching down like skeletal hands. The air thickened, a foul, earthy scent filling her nose, mingling with the coppery tang of blood. Her head felt heavy, her thoughts sluggish, as though something was seeping into her mind, clawing its way into her thoughts.

The spores. She could feel their effects creeping back, the numbness spreading through her limbs, slowing her movements. Her legs felt like lead, her arms hanging limply at her sides as she struggled to stay upright. The forest seemed to pulse around her, each shadow alive, watching her, waiting.

"Sarah..." she whispered, her voice barely audible, a desperate prayer to the friend she'd left behind.

But Sarah was gone. Claire was alone.

A flicker of movement caught her eye—a pale face, hollow and empty, floating between the trees. She blinked, and it was gone. But the image lingered, the face twisted in agony, eyes wide with a silent scream.

It was Ben.

She bit down on her lip, forcing herself to look away, to keep moving. The hallucinations were getting worse, the forest filling with the faces of her dead friends, haunting her with every step. She stumbled, her vision blurring as the spores took hold, her mind slipping into a fog. Her body felt heavy, her limbs numb, her breaths coming in shallow gasps.

"Claire..." A voice whispered from somewhere behind her, low and mocking. The teenage son's laughter followed, echoing through the trees, a chilling reminder of the danger closing in on her.

Claire forced herself forward, her heart pounding as she picked up speed, her feet slipping in the snow. Her mind raced, every instinct screaming that they were right behind her, closing in, ready to drag her back to that clearing, back to the horror she'd barely escaped.

But as she stumbled over a fallen branch, she heard the faint clinking of chains. The teenage son was close, his heavy footsteps crunching through the snow, each sound a reminder of the nightmare waiting to engulf her.

"You can't hide," he called, his voice dripping with sadistic pleasure. "I can smell you."

Claire's throat tightened, panic clawing at her chest. She forced herself to keep moving, each step heavy, her body fighting against the pull of the forest. The trees grew denser, their twisted branches reaching down, scraping against her skin as she pushed through, leaving thin red lines on her arms.

She stumbled around a tree and stopped short, her heart leaping into her throat. Standing in the middle of her path was the youngest child, her face eerily serene, her wide, dark eyes fixed on Claire with a disturbing innocence.

The child clutched something in her small hands, holding it up like a prized possession. Claire's stomach twisted as she realized what it was—Jake's severed head, his eyes vacant, his mouth open in a silent scream.

The child tilted her head, her lips curling into a small, eerie smile. "He's watching you," she whispered, her voice soft and lilting, like a lullaby. She lifted Jake's head, waving it slowly in front of Claire, her eyes gleaming with twisted amusement. "He can see everything you're doing."

Claire's legs shook, bile rising in her throat as she took a step back, her body screaming to run. She turned and bolted, the child's laughter ringing in her ears, a high-pitched, bone-chilling sound that echoed through the forest.

Claire didn't know how long she ran, her mind clouded with fear, her body moving on pure instinct. She crashed through the underbrush, her breath coming in gasps, her legs burning with every step. The trees began to thin, and she found herself at the edge of a steep cliff, the ground dropping away into a yawning chasm below.

She skidded to a stop, her chest heaving as she looked down, the mist swirling below, obscuring whatever lay at the bottom. Behind her, the sounds of the family's pursuit grew louder, their laughter and taunts filling the air, mingling with the cold wind that whipped through her hair.

The Matriarch stepped into view, her hulking form emerging from the shadows, her face twisted into a grin of dark satisfaction. She took a step closer, her eyes fixed on Claire with a gleam of triumph.

"Nowhere left to run," she purred, her voice soft and mocking. She gestured to her family, signaling them to stay back. This was her moment, her victory.

Claire backed up to the very edge of the cliff, her heart pounding as she looked down at the mist below. She knew what awaited her if she let them take her back—an agonizing, drawn-out death, her body torn apart piece by piece, feeding the family's sadistic hunger.

But there was another option.

COLD CUTS

The Matriarch took a step closer, her smile widening as she saw the fear in Claire's eyes. "Did you really think you could escape?" she sneered, her voice dripping with contempt. "The forest has claimed you, girl. It always gets what it wants."

Claire lifted her chin, her face set with grim determination. She met the Matriarch's gaze, defiance burning in her eyes, her voice steady as she spoke.

"You may own the forest," she said, her voice barely a whisper, "but you'll never own me."

Without another word, Claire turned and leapt from the cliff, her body plummeting into the mist below. The wind whipped past her face, cold and sharp, the forest's cries fading as she fell, her mind a blur of terror and relief.

The Matriarch watched as Claire disappeared into the mist, her face twisting in a mix of anger and satisfaction. She had wanted the girl alive, wanted to savor her terror, to hear her screams. But the forest was patient, and the forest would claim her body, one way or another.

She turned to her family, her expression cold and unyielding. "Leave her," she commanded, her voice low and final. "The forest will do what needs to be done."

The family nodded, their faces filled with dark satisfaction as they followed the Matriarch back into the trees, their laughter fading into the distance, leaving only the silent, waiting shadows of the forest.

As the family retreated, the forest fell into an eerie silence, the trees standing tall and watchful, their branches swaying in the cold wind. The spores drifted lazily through the air, settling over the cliff's edge like a shroud, their dark, malevolent presence a silent reminder of the forest's hunger.

Far below, the mist swirled, hiding whatever lay at the bottom of the cliff, concealing Claire's fate in its shadowy depths. The forest had claimed another soul, its hunger sated, if only for a moment.

But in the silence, there was a sense of waiting, a dark anticipation that hung over the forest like a curse. It would only be a matter of time before the forest called again, drawing in the lost, the desperate, and the unwary, luring them into its twisted depths.

And when they came, the forest would be waiting, its hunger eternal, its roots stretching deep into the earth, feeding on the fear and despair of those who wandered too close.

The spores drifted, settling into the trees, the ground, the air, silent sentinels of the forest's endless appetite.

Epilogue: Cold Cuts

THE FOREST LOOMED ON the horizon, a dense wall of green and shadow beneath the fading afternoon light. The air was crisp, filled with the earthy scent of fallen leaves and pine, as four figures walked along the dirt path leading into the trees.

"Come on, guys, you're killing my vibe," Darren called out, his voice carrying through the stillness as he adjusted the pack on his shoulder. He cast a grin over his shoulder at the others. "It's a camping trip, not a funeral march."

Beside him, Laura rolled her eyes, her lips pressed into a thin line. "Maybe if you actually helped carry something, you wouldn't have so much energy," she muttered, her tone dripping with irritation.

"Oh, come on. That's what you guys are here for," Darren replied, a smirk crossing his face. "Besides, I brought the important stuff." He reached into his pack and pulled out a loaf of bread and a bag of cold cuts, waving them in the air. "Sandwiches for days! And if we run out... we could always eat each other." He chuckled, throwing a wink at Laura.

One of the others, Jess, let out a nervous laugh, glancing around as though expecting someone to jump out from the shadows. "You're so morbid, Darren," she said, her voice wavering. "Can we not joke about cannibalism?"

Darren shrugged, tucking the bread and cold cuts back into his pack. "Relax, Jess. It's just a joke. Besides, this place is as quiet as a graveyard."

The group continued along the path, their voices fading into the quiet as they ventured deeper into the forest. The trees seemed to close in around them, their branches reaching down like silent sentinels, casting long shadows that danced across the ground. The air grew thick, and a strange, heavy silence settled over them, muffling their footsteps, as if the forest itself was holding its breath.

Jess slowed her pace, casting wary glances at the dense underbrush. "Is it just me, or is this place... creepy?" she whispered, her voice barely audible.

"Oh, come on, Jess," Darren scoffed, rolling his eyes. "It's a forest. Trees, dirt, squirrels—what's there to be scared of?"

Laura shot him a glare, irritation flashing in her eyes. "Maybe some of us don't enjoy being surrounded by things that could be hiding God-knows-what."

Darren opened his mouth to respond, but his words caught in his throat as a strange, sweet scent drifted through the air. It was faint, almost undetectable, yet it carried a weight that settled in their lungs, heavy and cloying.

"What is that smell?" Jess asked, wrinkling her nose.

"Probably just some rotting plants or something," Darren said dismissively. But even as he spoke, he felt an odd sensation creeping over him, a subtle heaviness in his limbs, as though the air itself was pressing down on him.

They continued in silence, the tension building as the trees grew denser, the shadows stretching longer. Laura stumbled over a root, cursing under her breath as she regained her balance.

But just as she looked up, her gaze caught on something in the distance—a small figure standing among the trees, partially obscured by shadow.

"Is that... a kid?" she murmured, squinting.

Jess turned to look, her eyes widening as she took in the figure. It was a little girl, her face pale and expressionless, her dark eyes fixed on them with an unnerving intensity. She raised her hand, waving slowly, her arm hanging at an odd angle.

"Wait..." Laura's voice trailed off, a chill running down her spine as she focused on the girl's hand. "That... that looks like an arm. Like... a real arm."

The others exchanged uneasy glances, shifting nervously as they watched the girl. Darren forced a laugh, though it sounded hollow in the thick silence. "Come on, it's just some kid playing a prank. Probably picked up a fake arm from a Halloween store."

But as they continued to watch, the little girl's expression remained blank, her eyes dark and empty, her arm—a severed limb—swaying in the breeze.

The group stood frozen, a deep, primal fear settling over them as they took in the sight. The forest seemed to close in around them, the shadows thickening, pressing down like a suffocating weight. And then, without a word, the girl turned and disappeared into the trees, leaving nothing but the silence and the faint, sickly sweet smell that lingered in the air.

A shiver ran through Jess as she backed away, her eyes darting between the trees. "I don't like this place," she whispered, her voice trembling. "I don't like it at all."

Darren forced a smile, trying to shake off the unease. "Oh, come on. It's just some kid messing with us." But his bravado rang hollow, the weight of the forest pressing down on him, seeping into his bones.

The air grew thick with spores, drifting lazily through the trees, settling on their clothes, their skin, as though the forest itself was marking them, welcoming them into its embrace. The scent of decay lingered, stronger now, filling their lungs with each breath, a sickly-sweet promise that clung to the air.

As they turned to leave, the forest seemed to whisper around them, the sound barely audible, a soft, mocking laughter that echoed through the trees. They glanced over their shoulders, a collective unease settling over them as they felt the unseen watchers in the shadows, eyes fixed on them, waiting.

The group pressed on, their footsteps quickening, their voices fading into the distance as they disappeared into the trees, leaving only the silence and the drifting spores behind.

The forest exhaled, its roots stretching deep, its hunger awakening as it welcomed its new guests. And in the shadows, unseen figures watched, their eyes gleaming with anticipation, waiting for the forest to claim what was rightfully its own.

Also by B. Humphrey

Retro Horrors: The Lost Decade
Cassette Ghosts
Summer of the Black Star
The Arcade Incident
Dead End Drive – In
The Polaroid Project
Endless Paths: The Choose-Your-Own Doom Chronicles
Neon Dreams
The Forgotten Carnival
Satanic Panic
Skin of the Moon

The Autumn Folklore Chronicles
The Forest Of Forgotten Names
The Witch Of Windspindle Hollow
The Burrowfolk Chronicles

The Phantom Finders Club

A Haunting On Maplewood Street
The Secrets Of Old Fort Tower
Ghosts OF The Infirmary

The Starling Sleuths
Detective Starling vol. 1
Detective Starling Vol. 2

Winter Horrors
Whispers of the Wendigo
Cold Cuts

Standalone
The Witch of Blackwood Hollow

Milton Keynes UK
Ingram Content Group UK Ltd.
UKHW032222231124
451423UK00014B/1276